Luz

A play

By

Catherine Filloux

NoPassport Press

ne Filloux

2014 by Catherine Filloux.

Luz by Catherine Filloux

Copyright 2012, 2014 by Catherine Filloux.

For performance inquiries contact:
Elaine Devlin Literary Inc., 411 Lafayette Street,
6th Flr, NY, NY 10003. Phone: 212-842-9030, email:
edevlinlit@aol.com
Or author at www.catherinefilloux.com

NoPassport Press Dreaming the Americas Series

PO Box 1786, South Gate CA 90280 USA

NoPassportPress@aol.com, www.nopassport.org

ISBN: 978-1-312-20614-4

Luz: Catherine Filloux's Necessary Theatre

By José Zayas

I first met Catherine when she approached me after seeing my production of Caridad Svich's play _The House of the Spirits_, based on the Isabel Allende novel, at Repertorio Espanol in 2009. She told me that she was impressed by the scale of the work and was wondering if I might be interested in working with her on a project. I knew of her work as a playwright and an activist and was intrigued by the prospect of collaborating with her on something. Though my work as a director had always seemed to have a political dimension I'd never considered myself to have a particular political agenda and it was with great excitement that I began to work with Catherine on the play that was originally called _Action Hero_ - I was awed by the scope of what she was trying to achieve and I felt that working on her play was a natural extension of the work that I'd been exploring over the past couple of years - creating epic work on an intimate scale. The play shifted, found a focus, changed its name and eventually became what is now being published. It was an exhilarating process and I count myself very lucky to have been part of it.

On the surface _Luz_ is about Alexandra, an American human rights lawyer, and her relationship with a series of clients from different parts of the world

3

including the Sudan, Haiti and Guatemala. It begins as a procedural moving swiftly in and out of different offices like an episode of "Law and Order" introducing its characters and themes in a clear and concise language, unadorned and unsentimental, but as it progresses the play begins to widen its scope and what at first appears to be small and intimate becomes much larger and harder to pin down. We are also introduced to Oliver, the head of public relations for a big oil company dealing with a devastating oil spill. Alexandra and Oliver's stories intersect throughout but the characters never meet. These parallel stories are provocatively brought together in a work that takes a hard look at gender based violence on a global scale and makes shocking connections between corporate and human rights law practices. It's an intelligent, passionate and fiercely political play that never loses its narrative drive and refuses to polemicize or victimize any of its characters ultimately revealing itself to be a large scale work, panoramic in its view of its subject and people, poetic and surreal, tender and violent but always clear eyed and hopeful.

The first image Catherine asks us to consider is that of a laughing judge. The Law is in uproar, it has turned inside out, it has been corrupted and it is terrifying. Alexandra's client Zia, has undergone a series of devastating encounters within the U.S. court system that have left her empty and cynical and she is now afraid of the very system that she once thought would help her. Alexandra responds by saying "The law is better than this"- the rest of the play will ask us to consider this statement and look at it from different perspectives. Onstage, it's a throwaway line, a moment of reassurance, a platitude perhaps, but it is the engine that drives this play. Alexandra has to believe this in order to do what she does - the system is broken but it is not irreparable. She needs to begin with hope in order to delve into the darkness that surrounds all of her clients. And this is the same hope that drives Catherine as a theater maker. She is a poet of the possible but has taken on the daunting task of documenting behavior that to those of us who are not living in the battle scarred landscapes of her characters seems impossible. The crimes she writes about are not supposed to be talked about in fact it would be better if they remained "secrets"- in interviews she has said that they are:

" ...the best-kept secrets, but they're not even secrets. They happen all the time, and nobody cares. And that's the problem on some level with doing this kind of theater. There's just a little wall that's been built up against these things, and to write theater about them is part of the challenge."

Audiences do build walls when faced with unabashedly political work, and make no mistake

Catherine's work is Political, she is a tireless activist engaged not only through her writing but through her actions - the process of writing for Catherine isn't a solitary venture, as she is writing she thinks about the people who she wants to engage in dialogue, she reaches out and makes them come together in unexpected ways - during the process of developing *Luz* we did a wonderful reading at CultureHub where all of the characters who were from Guatemala were actually read by actors IN Guatemala - technology allowed us to listen to the text in a completely new way, even though we were thousands of miles apart we were able to share in a deep experience that enriched our understanding of the play and more importantly allowed us to have a direct conversation with a Guatemalan audience.

Catherine understands that we don't come to the theater to be lectured. We want to see something alive, something vital. To witness, that is her goal, to make us witness, to reveal to us what we are not supposed to know, to make us feel (Empathy) and to make us question what we thought we already knew. She achieves this by creating a world that lures you in with its procedural set up and then envelopes you in the inner landscapes of its characters - dreams, songs, jokes, language shifts, puppets, unexpected connections and schisms abound making for a thoroughly involving and involved 85 minutes. The play finds resolution in its dreams, not in the law, in the connections that the characters make in non literal spaces. The law fails the women because it asks them to define their traumas in terms that are too narrow, too literal and too self serving. Catherine's play uses that idea as the jumping off point to then engage us in a multitude of possible questions: How is trauma recognized? How is trauma stored in the body? Is it in the body? Is it in our language? Is it in our dreams? And who really gets to define this?

The play does not provide any answers.

It creates the space for Inquiry.

For Debate.

For Outrage.

And for Hope.

LUZ

A Play

By Catherine Filloux

LUZ was presented by La MaMa in New York City
At La MaMa's First Floor Theatre
September 28 thru October 14, 2012

LUZ
A Watson Arts Project
By **Catherine Filloux**
Directed by **José Zayas**

Music Composed by **Sergio R. Reyes**
Set Design by **Maruti Evans**
Lighting Design by **Yi Zhao**
Costume Design by **Carla Bellisio**
Sound Design by **David Margolin Lawson**
Puppet Design by **Emily DeCola** and **The Puppet Kitchen**
Puppeteers: **Chloe Moser** and **Kiku Sakai**
Digital Music Production: **Michael Sirotta**
Digital Music Production of 'Lullaby': **Yukio Tsuji**
Production Stage Manager: **Shannon O'Neil**
Assistant Director: **Jon Burklund**
Assistant Stage Manager: **Katie Meade**
Production Assistants:
Ellen Goldberg, Molly Haas-Hooven, Suzanne Karpinski, Chloe Lewis

Watson Arts Project: **Mary Fulham**
Press Representation: **Sam Rudy Media Relations**

CAST
(IN ORDER OF APPEARANCE):

Alexandra: Kimber Riddle*
Zia/Yvonne/Daniela/Judge Hurst: Kim Brockington
Oliver: Steven Rishard*
Haskins/Jesus/Roasted Swan: Bobby Plasencia*
Judge Taylor/Matthew Cameron/Guard/Mr.
Colby/Reporter: Peter Jay Fernandez*
Abuelita: Teresa Yenque*
Luz: Julissa Roman
Norton/Helene/Carmen Ramos: Lynnette R. Freeman*

*Members of Actors' Equity Association

The play runs approximately 85 minutes without an intermission.

Special Thanks: Tea Alagic, Darien Bates, Taina Bien-Aime, Magda Bogin, Patricia Caswell: The Hermitage Artist Retreat, Billy Clark/Culturehub, Kia Corthron, John Daggett, Dalia Davi, Francis DelDuca, Liz Diamond, Mustafa Eljaili, Dominique Filloux, Fordham University (Elizabeth Margid and Dawn Saito), Denise Greber, Stephen Haff, Lanna Joffrey, Joyce Isabelle, Adam Kraar, Sarah Lederman, Samantha Leigh, Jessica Litwak, Especianise Loresca, Melissa Maxwell, Mary McLaughlin, Lindsey Medeiros, Aleksander Milch, Santo Mollica, Alfredo Narciso, New School (Kathy Rossetter and Bob

Hoyt), Ayesha Ngaujah, Lynn Nottage, NYU/Gallatin, Natalie Osborne, Beverly Petty, Tim Pracher-Dix, Megan Pries, Akili Prince, Heather Raffo, Gordana Rashovich, James Reynolds, Jesse Ricke, Lorena Rodas, Jay O. Sanders, Sanaa, Toni Shapiro-Phim, Helga Shepard, Jane Stanicki, Sarah Cameron Sunde, JudyTate, Teatro Abril, Leslie Timko, Joe Urla, Jurrien Westerhof, Connie Winston, Janice Wormington, Mia Yoo and Merina Zulianie.

LUZ was produced by special arrangement with the Playwright and Elaine Devlin Literary, Inc.

LUZ is dedicated to AH.
***

Cast of Characters:

(5 females/3 males)
(In order of appearance)

1) Alexandra, *an American human rights lawyer, 40s*
2) Zia, *Alexandra's client from the Sudan*
Yvonne, *Helene's friend from Haiti*
Daniela, *Oliver's wife*
3) Oliver, *head of public relations for an oil company*
4) Haskins, *a corporate lawyer at Alexandra's law firm*
Jesus, *a gang member in Guatemala City*
Roasted Swan, *a male singer in "Carmina Burana," who haunts Oliver*
5) Judge Taylor, *the judge on Zia's case*
Matthew Cameron, *an environmental activist*
Guard, *a prison guard in Haiti*
Mr. Colby, *government lawyer on Luz's case*
Reporter
6) *Abuelita, Luz's grandmother*
Judge Hurst, *the judge on Luz's case*
7) Luz, *Alexandra's client, a Guatemalan refugee, 40s*
8) Norton, *the government lawyer on Zia's case*
Helene, *Alexandra's client from Haiti*
Carmen Ramos, *a Guatemalan human rights activist*
Vulture (Puppet)

SCENE 1:

(Alexandra, an American human rights lawyer is in her office with Zia, her client from the Sudan.)

ZIA: He is laughing at me. I dream about it all the time.

ALEXANDRA: Judge Taylor?

ZIA: Yes, Sharia law was imposed on us--I was *forced* to wear a headscarf. "It must have been a very ugly scarf," he laughed. He was laughing so hard. He said it was a "comic moment."

ALEXANDRA: I chose to appeal your case because I read what he did to you. The law is better than this.

ZIA: Thank you, but I cannot face him again. I thought I wanted asylum, but now the idea of seeing him, I can't.

ALEXANDRA: Tell me about your life, Zia.

ZIA: I'm a runner. I'm a historian. Right now, I work in DC analyzing satellite pictures from Darfur. The violence never seems to end. I have been waiting for years for a decision. Hanging in this kind of strange in-between place. Not allowed to stay, too afraid to return to a country that will target me. Who am I? Miss In-Between.

ALEXANDRA: I read what happened to you in court the first time, and I knew that it was unjust.

ZIA: And you, Alexandra Stevens, can make it just?

ALEXANDRA: This is a big corporate law firm. I'm the pro bono counsel. You don't have to worry about

Judge Taylor laughing at you. He'll be too embarrassed because I had him reprimanded.

ZIA: How?

ALEXANDRA: I wrote to the court of appeals. If you can trust me, even though we just met today, we can do this together. My business is the business of paper. So much paper. But there's meaning in all the words, if you know how to use them. And words stand for behavior. Good and bad behavior. Law moves one slow step at a time. Like a turtle.

ZIA: A crippled turtle.

ALEXANDRA: The government lawyer on your case is a die-hard. I called her to see if she'd settle out of court but she's sinking her teeth in till she's forced to say, "Uncle."

ZIA: Whose uncle?

ALEXANDRA: It's just an expression.

ZIA: What if the judge has an uncle and he is there too, laughing? Two laughing judges. That's a nightmare.

ALEXANDRA: (Laughing.) There will be only one judge. And the government lawyer won't have much to say, you'll see. It's late--you should get back to your hotel. Get some sleep.

ZIA: I will be up all night. Do you know what it is like to lie in the dark and stare up at the terror of not knowing. Will I go back to school way too late in life and learn what I need to learn? Will I ever see my home again? Will the torture be too hard to bear?

ALEXANDRA: What would help, Zia?

ZIA: Running but it is dark outside.

SCENE 2:

(Oliver, the head of public relations for an oil company, prepares to leave his office, as a corporate lawyer, Tim Haskins, shows him photos on his phone.)

OLIVER: A thousand swans is the price we have to pay for civilization, Haskins.

HASKINS: It's a bit more than a thousand. And other birds are involved.

OLIVER: Ducks. Who cares?

HASKINS: Well, apparently the indigenous people who are suing you.

OLIVER: Stop showing me those pictures!

HASKINS: It's hard to tell the bird muck from the oil muck.

OLIVER: Since when do people who scratch pictures in rocks have digital cameras? It's that asshole Matthew Cameron! This is an environmental activist who uses tons of jet fuel to fly around the world on a lecture tour.

HASKINS: Well regardless, he's branded himself in a way everyone loves.

OLIVER: My son Mike loves him. He hates *me*. The hypocrisy.

HASKINS: Your son's?

OLIVER: Teenagers are allowed to be hypocrites, Haskins! The shareholders. They want profits and political correctness. Fuckers. That's between you and me.

HASKINS: Of course, Mr. Rausch. The complaints are coming out of the woodwork. There are air and water contamination issues...

OLIVER: Right and it's *your* job to settle with them, so I can do *my* job.

HASKINS: Talk to me about the Fake Vulture.

OLIVER: You didn't read my pamphlet *Issues and Opportunities*?

HASKINS: It looks like one of those oversized birds on a merry-go-round.

OLIVER: Small amounts of bitumen can create patches of oil on the surface of tailings facilities.

HASKINS: Tailings facilities? You mean the oil slicks?

OLIVER: We call them "tailings facilities"! If birds were to land...

HASKINS: They did land.

OLIVER: To minimize the risk we have implemented an over-sized mechanical vulture with flapping wings and speakers emitting bird-of-prey calls.

HASKINS: Okay, great, I'll read your pamphlet more carefully, so I can explain it to the indigenous people. They worship birds, they're sacred--"Sky-Gods." They don't understand the Fake Vulture.

OLIVER: Sky-Gods? I don't want to hear another word about swans. This is a tempest in a teapot.

HASKINS: Or a swan in a cesspool.

OLIVER: Haskins, you do understand how important these new reserves in Latin America are, yes?

HASKINS: Yes, Mr. Rausch, I understand that. Now about Matthew Cameron--how much has the volume of letters truly increased?

OLIVER: Enough to fill a conference room. At first they were mostly from Montana, now they're coming from around the world.

(Oliver shows him a pile of mail.)

OLIVER: Matthew Cameron's calling it "The Last Letter Writing Campaign on Earth." That's his shtick. Kids draw pictures of things like the ozone layer. Lots of gray and green. They even put X's and O's for hugs and kisses. You know, kids.

HASKINS: They still say the same things about dead birds?

OLIVER: Everyone is getting a personal response. I want to talk to Matthew Cameron, face to face.

HASKINS: After you deal with the swan debacle you fly to...?

OLIVER: "Victory," not "debacle," Haskins! Our bird deterrent system is rated best in class. After, I fly to L.A.--Daniela's singing *Carmina Burana*! You know (Singing) "Semper crescis aut decrescis..." *O Fortuna*, they use it in movies.

HASKINS: So I'll arrange the meeting with Matthew Cameron when you get back.

OLIVER: (Starting to go.) Hey, I'm a "Sky-God" too. I live on airplanes.

SCENE 3:

(Alexandra and Zia face Judge Stewart Taylor. The government lawyer, Gina Norton, is nearby.)

JUDGE TAYLOR: Do you swear that everything you'll say is true and nothing but the truth so help you god?

ZIA: Yes, Your Honor.

JUDGE TAYLOR: Please be seated. Do you want Attorney Stevens to represent you?

ZIA: Yes.

(Judge Taylor examines a stack of paper and laughs.)

JUDGE TAYLOR: This is an awfully large packet of materials you have brought in today, counsel. And quite an extended affidavit. Don't you want to save trees?

ALEXANDRA: Understood, Your Honor.

JUDGE TAYLOR: We are now up to Exhibit 17 and...18.

ZIA: (Whispering to Alexandra.) He knows how to count.

JUDGE TAYLOR: Counsel, do you object to any of the documents that are being admitted into evidence?

NORTON: No, not at this time, Your Honor. I will have some questions for the respondent.

JUDGE TAYLOR: Why did you file so many legal briefs, declarations and documents, counsel?

ALEXANDRA: Your Honor, these exhibits are necessary to be included in the record.

JUDGE TAYLOR: Why?

ALEXANDRA: To document the actual facts of the case.

JUDGE TAYLOR: What do you mean?

ALEXANDRA: My petition for review outlines that Ms. Zia Mahdi's shame was the basis for not giving all the details to you the first time she was in court. Your Honor, there are precedents for that. The record states that you asked her why she was embarrassed to see a doctor after she was raped. She told no one in her country about the rape. She was ashamed. It's documented that she left the country to have surgery. She lost her memory at times when she was being tortured but her statements have never been contradictory. She says the torture in the security center, which is referred to in her testimony as the "ghost house," began when they overthrew her party. She refused to sign a confession saying she gave out anti-government propaganda because she knew the punishment under Islamic law was *death*. Our country report shows the persecution of political opponents if she returns and conditions have gotten even worse. She showed her scars to you.

(Zia holds out her hands.)

ALEXANDRA: Denying her asylum the first time, you ignored the fact of her scars. She was forced to sit on a piece of broken glass as the record states and you asked her how many hours. We have documentation here that it was for three hours at a time. And if you recall you responded to her testimony about being forced to conform to Sharia law dress codes by

laughing at her. These exhibits are included today should another appeal prove to be necessary.
JUDGE TAYLOR: (Laughing self-consciously.) Give me a minute here.
ALEXANDRA: Yes, Your Honor.

(*Judge Taylor arranges the papers in a neat stack.*)

JUDGE TAYLOR: It won't be.
ALEXANDRA: Your Honor?
JUDGE TAYLOR: The respondent presents a credible and well-documented case. I am satisfied that the facts point to torture and further persecution if she returns to her country. My decision is to grant the respondent asylum. Ms. Norton, do you wish to reserve appeal on any issue?
NORTON: The Service waives appeal, Your Honor.
JUDGE TAYLOR: Thank you very much. Here, then is my written order memorializing the final decision of this court.

(*He signs, hole punches and hands Norton two copies of the signed decision.*)

JUDGE TAYLOR: Counselor, could you be so kind as to serve Ms. Stevens with a copy of my decision.

(*Norton hands the decision to Alexandra.*)

ALEXANDRA: Thank you, Your Honor.

JUDGE TAYLOR: Thank you both.

(*Judge Taylor and Norton exit. Zia shakes Alexandra's hand.*)

ALEXANDRA: "Uncle"!

SCENE 4:

(*The lawyer, Tim Haskins, is in Alexandra's office.*)

HASKINS: An *alien* cannot work at McDonald's, Alexa.
ALEXANDRA: She is an "undocumented worker." No one who seeks our services is an *alien*. Please do not use the word "alien."
HASKINS: She broke my trust.
ALEXANDRA: How did she "break your trust?"
HASKINS: She doesn't have a work permit.
ALEXANDRA: Lots of people don't. She has the right to work so she can eat and put a roof over her head. Why are you going by the book like this? I assigned this case to you because I thought you could handle it.
HASKINS: They dumped the "swan lawsuit" in my lap. I've got five people working on it--I'm buried!
ALEXANDRA: I need to fly to Haiti for a humanitarian parole case. And I don't have time to take this on too.
HASKINS: There's bound to be a junior who can take over.

21

ALEXANDRA: Yeah, someone else who will treat her as an *alien*.

HASKINS: Okay, I got it!

ALEXANDRA: Why did you volunteer?

HASKINS: Wanted to help out. And it made my mother happy I was doing pro bono work.

ALEXANDRA: Oh, you did it for your mother? Let me tell you something, it's not about Ms. Lopez breaking *your* trust. It's about Ms. Lopez *needing* your trust. Do you realize what's at stake for her?

HASKINS: Of course! Why are you talking to me this way?

ALEXANDRA: She has lost everything. Have you read her file? Now it's going to be even worse for her than when we started. You think she'll go back to McDonald's after you scared her? How is she supposed to live? She had the guts to seek us out. Ms. Lopez is in there waiting but you'd rather defend killing birds in oil slicks.

HASKINS: "Tailings facilities."

ALEXANDRA: Just give me her file!

HASKINS: I'm in this 24-7.

ALEXANDRA: It's fine, Tim.

HASKINS: I don't have a choice.

ALEXANDRA: I'll take care of it.

(Luz, a Guatemalan refugee, waits in a chair in a law firm conference room. Alexandra joins Luz.)

ALEXANDRA: Thank you for waiting, Ms. Lopez, I'm sorry. I'm taking over your case. I'm your new lawyer, Alexandra Stevens. Please call me Alexandra. I know that we have just met each other, but I need you to tell me your story so that I can help you. I have hope that you can win asylum. May I call you Luz?

(Luz nods.)

ALEXANDRA: Can you tell me some of your good memories…? What do you remember about your native village…? You're here, not in Guatemala. You're with me…What makes you feel safe?
LUZ: (Softly.) I collected black salt with my abuelita in the village.
ALEXANDRA: You collected salt with your grandmother?

(Luz nods.)

ALEXANDRA: Where did the salt come from?
LUZ: (Searching for the word in English, but she can't find it.) Posos sagrados.
ALEXANDRA: Wells. Sacred wells.
LUZ: My chest hurts.
ALEXANDRA: We'll get you a doctor for your asthma, and medicine. I know that you had to flee your village during the civil war, Luz. Where did you go after that?

LUZ: To the mountains. Abuelita knew we had to escape. Then we needed money, we went to the basurero.

ALEXANDRA: You lived in the garbage dump. In Guatemala City?

LUZ: Yes, we collected plastic. We stayed with her cousin, the mother of Jesus.

ALEXANDRA: Who is Jesus?

(Luz coughs as lights shift to Luz with Jesus in the dump. Luz and Jesus speak in Spanish. Supertitles are used. Alexandra remains in the scenes.)

JESUS: Tomá mi bufanda. (Take my handkerchief.)

LUZ: El aire me provoca asma. (The air gives me asthma.)

JESUS: Es el metano. (It's the methane.)

LUZ: Alguien tiró un cigarro, deberías haber visto lo rápido que se expandió el fuego, y explotó! Hasta me quemó el brazo. Mirá, encontré esto ayer. (Somebody dropped a cigarette--you should have seen how fast a fire exploded! I got burned on my arm. I found this, though, yesterday.)

(She shows him a ring, which he takes.)

JESUS: Hmm. Oro! (Gold!)

LUZ: Devolvémelo. (Give it back.)

(He doesn't give it back.)

LUZ: Devolvémelo! (Give it back!)

(She wrestles it from him.)

LUZ: Voy a venderlo, voy a comprar ropa nueva y a buscar trabajo. (I'm going sell it, buy new clothes, and find a job.)

JESUS: ¿Te gusta mi nuevo tatuaje? (Like my new tattoo?)

(She looks at a tattoo on his forearm.)

LUZ: ¿Qué es? (What is it?)

JESUS: Centroamérica. Estamos recuperándola. (Centroamérica. We're taking it back.)

LUZ: Recuperando qué? (Taking what back?)

JESUS: Lo que es nuestro. (What's ours.)

LUZ: Como van a recuperarlo? (How can you take it back?)

JESUS: Controlamos la gasolinera, Lucita! (We control their big gas station, Lucita!)

LUZ: Cual gasolinera? (What gas station?)

JESUS: (Pointing.) Viste las bellisimas puertas del cielo en la cima del basurero? (You've seen the beautiful gates of heaven at the top of the dump?)

LUZ: Que bellisimas puertas del cielo? (What beautiful gates of heaven?)

JESUS: La gasolinera, nuestra zona! Tenemos negocios en la gasolinera. (The gas station, our turf! We do business at the gas station.)

LUZ: Vendés drogas en la gasolinera. (You sell drugs at the gas station.)

JESUS: Los Estados Unidos mantienen nuestro negocio. (Picking her up in his arms.) Si estuvieras con nosotros, te protegeríamos. Adiós al asma! (The United States keeps us in business. If you're with us, we'll protect you. No more asthma where we are.)

LUZ: Voy tarde a clases. (I'm late for class.)

JESUS: (Laughing.) Clases de inglés? Te tienen comiendo de su mano. (English class? They have you eating right out of their hands.)

LUZ: Tu hablás ingles. (You speak English.)

JESUS: Hay que conocer al enemigo. (Know your enemy.)

LUZ: Soló traéle la leche a la abuelita. (Just bring abuelita her milk.)

JESUS: Le traje comida a tú mascota. (I brought you some grain for your pet.)

LUZ: Gracias. (Thank you.)

JESUS: Cómo sigue su pata? (How's her leg?)

LUZ: Casi curada totalmente. (Almost healed.)

JESUS: Después, vas a dejarla libre? (Then you'll let her go?)

LUZ: No. Mi pequeñita se quedará con nosotros. (No. My little one will stay with us.)

JESUS: Los zopes nascieron para volar. (Vultures are meant to fly.)

LUZ: Ella quiere quedarse con nosotros. Se siente segura conmigo. (She likes us. She feels safe with me.)

JESUS: Voy a pintar tu nombre en la pared de la gasolinera. Y al lado de tu nombre voy a pintar un corazón. Y en ese corazón voy a poner un sol. Y en ese sol voy a poner una llama. (I'm going to graffiti your name on the side of the gas station. And next to your name I'm going to put a heart. And in that heart I'm going to put the sun. And in that sun I'm going to put a flame.)

LUZ: Los poetas van a la escuela. (Poets go to school.)

JESUS: Acá no, muñeca. (Not here, baby doll.)

(Lights shift.)

ALEXANDRA: Then you found a job as a domestic in Guatemala City. The man who employed you…that's the reason you can't go back.

LUZ: Yes…I want to send money to my abuelita but I had to leave my job at McDonald's.

ALEXANDRA: We'll help you find another one, I promise.

LUZ: But Mr. Haskins, he said that…

ALEXANDRA: Mr. Haskins was wrong--it's okay.

LUZ: He gave me chocolate the first day. He said it was from his mother.

ALEXANDRA: That was very nice, of his mother. Was it good?

LUZ: With nuts.

ALEXANDRA: I'm sorry I didn't bring you any.

LUZ: It is never too late.

27

SCENE 5:

(Oliver in his office meets with the environmentalist, Matthew Cameron.)

OLIVER: Matthew Cameron in the flesh. Your letter campaign is making quite a splash.

MATTHEW: Mr. Haskins said it was urgent and I was on my way east anyway. Not that I like cities.

OLIVER: First, Mr. Cameron, let me say I share all your ideas. My son is all about the turtle eggs in Florida. The turtles are nearly extinct. Some oil from a spill reached them. It's in the DNA of the eggs. I'm very proud of him--he challenges me all the time about global warming.

MATTHEW: Call me Matthew.

OLIVER: I personally am very interested in wave power as a source of renewable energy. And Mr. Cameron we've just opened 25 wind farms totaling 3000 megawatts.

MATTHEW: Mr. Rausch, it's just a *snail mail* campaign. You know about the stamp called "Forever"?

OLIVER: Customers need fuel and we try to supply that in the safest way possible.

MATTHEW: I wondered if you knew about the stamp the U.S. postal service issued?

(Oliver stares at Matthew blankly.)

MATTHEW: The "Forever" stamp?

OLIVER: Yes!

MATTHEW: So you know the cost of a stamp keeps rising so fast they don't put a number on it anymore, that means snail mail is dead. We are at the end of the epistolary road.

OLIVER: I think it's a shame that letters went the way of the phonograph, Mr. Cameron. I am one who keeps LPs. I have large shelves dedicated to them, as does my wife.

MATTHEW: Who is an opera singer. I heard she'll be singing *Carmina Burana* at Carnegie Hall. You met her, in fact, when you sang in the *amateur* chorus years ago. You're a singing family.

OLIVER: Not anymore. You know a lot about my family.

MATTHEW: And I was impressed to learn you own one of the orange Mark Rothkos. But the point is, you're killing the planet.

OLIVER: Mr. Cameron, *I* am not killing the planet and you know that. You like Rothko?

MATTHEW: I do, but the letter campaign is really just a swan song--forgive the pun--to the belief that--in the time it took a letter to reach the other person--the message was still important enough, that it hadn't already switched to a new sound-byte.

OLIVER: How do you measure success, Matthew? When is it over?

MATTHEW: When the people decide.

OLIVER: What if nothing changes?

MATTHEW: Try something new.

OLIVER: Something more violent like your books describe?

MATTHEW: It's a movement already in motion. Separate from me. It got picked up by Twitter, and Tweeter, and Twister...

OLIVER: Isn't that paradoxical given your love for the epistolary.

MATTHEW: Yes but it's the *message* that's important. OIL IS NOT SUSTAINABLE. Black blood.

OLIVER: Let's be intelligent.

MATTHEW: Let's.

OLIVER: Mr. Cameron, we do our work as well as we can, and climate change, especially, worries *me* very much.

MATTHEW: I know. You used to work as a water scientist. What happened?

OLIVER: I got involved in defending some water pollution issues. People needed me elsewhere. I've always believed, go where the need is. And the money.

MATTHEW: You must need a lot of security and white noise to sleep at night.

OLIVER: I'd like you to take a look at this report.

MATTHEW: I'd love to.

OLIVER: Share your comments with me...

MATTHEW: (Looking at report.) Oh, here's the best-in-class bird deterrent. How would *you* like to be flapping your wings home, Mr. Rausch, on a time clock created by primordial nature itself? Only to be harshly jolted from your migration by a man-made plastic knock off of a vulture that passive-aggressively assaults you with strobe lights and digitally-activated squawks?

OLIVER: Soon we're going to have to pay for the swans' psychiatric bills.

MATTHEW: Sure, I'll share my comments: I'm stuck with a bunch of colored pie charts and a promo DVD, meanwhile you're lobbying for drilling rights and pipeline construction in South America, giving money to museum X and orchestra Y, and to fossil energy lobby groups with names like Sound Science Foundation. I can keep going if you'd like…

OLIVER: I see you use the same long parenthetical sentences when you speak.

MATTHEW: You read my books.

OLIVER: No, bullet-points. (Checking his phone.) Oh, a reason to smile, it's my wife. (On phone.) Hey Daniela, you have a fan here…Matthew Cameron. I'm taking your lead and eating a raw egg yolk for my voice…Okay, I'll call you later, babe. (Hangs up.) It's a lubricant. I'm shooting a shareholders' webcast.

MATTHEW: You're getting a sore throat from "the spin", Mr. Rausch. Yes, I've seen the glossy spreads in the biz magazines where they've christened you "the guru of oil." Say no to the big bastion of insanity that shines in the rutted roads of all the world's poorest countries—massive cleanups are needed not *gas stations*.

OLIVER: You don't have children.

MATTHEW: Thank god.

OLIVER: But something changes, and then you have to protect them.

MATTHEW: Against the rape of the planet.

OLIVER: People get put in jail.

MATTHEW: That's how they get silenced. I'm not about silence.

SCENE 6:

(Alexandra enters her office. She looks up at a narrow window, where a beam of light streams through. Luz enters. She speaks in Spanish, supertitles are used.)

LUZ: Mi abuelita dice que cuando una mujer ha sido violada, su alma no atravesará la estrecha ventana hacia el cielo, y volverá a la tierra como el viento que sopla la milpa en tiempos de rosa. (Abuelita said that when a woman has been raped, her soul can't get to heaven through the narrow window, and will return to earth as wind that blows over the cornfield at the times of burning.)

ALEXANDRA: You get to heaven through a narrow window?

(Luz points up at the narrow window with the beam of light.)

LUZ: Como esa. Cualquier mujer como yo, que ha sido violada no puede entrar. Ven conmigo,

Alexandra, cuando te quemen. (Like that one. Anyone like me who has been raped can't get in. Come with me, Alexandra, when they burn you.)

ALEXANDRA: Where?

LUZ: Sobre la milpa. Oscuras como carbón. (Over the cornfield. Dark as charcoal.)

ALEXANDRA: You have to run without your shoes.

LUZ: Cuando el techo explote sobre tu cabeza…(When the ceiling explodes above your head…)

ALEXANDRA: You have to hide under the ground.

LUZ: Como zanahoria creciendo debajo de la tierra. (Like a carrot growing downward.)

ALEXANDRA: Down the rabbit hole.

(Alexandra looks up at the narrow window. Luz exits as lights shift back to Alexandra's office.)

ALEXANDRA: I'm dreaming.

SCENE 7:

(Alexandra enters a jail cell in Haiti where her client, Helene, stands behind a Guard. The Guard allows Helene to go to Alexandra and Helene hugs her.)

HELENE: Alexandra, we heard rumors that they would take us in at Turks and Caicos.

GUARD: Well, the rumors were wrong.

HELENE: There were so many of us packed on that boat, so much shoving and then Yvonne's baby fell from her arms!

GUARD: And then this idiot has to jump off the boat and cause a near calamity. They had to haul her back up from the sea with a rope. The captain is still talking about it. She almost didn't make it.

HELENE: I learned to swim from my mother! She learned from her mother! Could I let that baby drown?

GUARD: But it *did* drown, you fool.

HELENE: The sea was too agitated. I held poor Yvonne like this. And she said to me the sea is my baby's tomb now.

ALEXANDRA: I'm her lawyer--you can release her to me.

GUARD: She broke the law!

ALEXANDRA: She has humanitarian parole pending in the U.S. I'm legally responsible for her safety, sir.

GUARD: She should not have tried to escape to Turks and Caicos and expect to be allowed back into Haiti. She is being detained!

ALEXANDRA: Detained in her own country?

GUARD: She left it.

ALEXANDRA: Had they allowed her to stay in Turks and Caicos she would have.

GUARD: *Some* of the women were allowed to stay.

ALEXANDRA: Yes, and they were put in jail there. Those were the choices. Jail or back to Haiti.

GUARD: She forsook her home. She left illegally.

ALEXANDRA: She has diabetes--she'll die here without proper treatment.

HELENE: (Singing; overlapping.) *"Chak maten, lè solèy la leve."* (Creole Pronunciations at end.)

ALEXANDRA: (Overlapping over singing.) She needs to come with me, now.

HELENE: We sang it on the boat. It's a song of solidarity! *"Nan fenèt mwen…"*

GUARD: STOP SINGING!

ALEXANDRA: She's protected by the United States.

HELENE: *"Map gade lanmè a…"*

GUARD: The United States has proved useless as far as I see…!

HELENE: *"Mwen se manman lanmè a…"*

ALEXANDRA: I will not leave this jail.

GUARD: You have sold Haiti to the devil!

HELENE: *"Chak maten, lè solèy la leve."*

ALEXANDRA: (Overlapping with singing.) You need to release her!

HELENE: *"Bebe mwen!"*

GUARD: STOP SINGING!

HELENE: *"Bebe mwen!"*

ALEXANDRA: I'm making some phone calls.

(*The guard looks at Alexandra's phone.*)

GUARD: Just get out of here. Both of you.

(*He exits and they leave, going outside.*)

ALEXANDRA: He had no right to detain you.

HELENE: No. Will this ruin my case in America, Alexandra?

ALEXANDRA: The grounds for your case are here you can't get treatment for diabetes.

HELENE: The "sugar disease." Our ancestors died making the white people sugar.

ALEXANDRA: But don't take another boat.

HELENE: I had to go, Alexandra, because I am getting threats, everyday.

ALEXANDRA: What do they say?

HELENE: "Your mother is part of that group."

ALEXANDRA: What "group?"

HELENE: The group of women who turn in the men who rape. "Where's your mother? She's telling the police lies." I tell them she died in the earthquake-- she's gone. "And where's your grandmother? She started the troublemaking!" My grandmother was raped in the prior regime. She gave the women whistles to blow when they were in danger. She died when the dictator's army descended like dogs.

ALEXANDRA: We have to wait for the medical declarations that you need dialysis, then we'll have to find you a sponsor. All the ducks have to be lined up in a row.

HELENE: What ducks?

ALEXANDRA: All the little bureaucratic ducks. I mean, the paperwork, the forms, the money to guarantee that you'll be accounted for.

HELENE: (Suspiciously.) What does that mean "accounted for?"

ALEXANDRA: It means money to guarantee you won't be a burden to the state.

HELENE: "Burden to what state?" There are 50.

ALEXANDRA: You ask good questions. You'd make a good lawyer.

HELENE: You think so?

ALEXANDRA: You'll get the world to stop eating sugar. Everyone will be skinny.

HELENE: I will be President one day.

ALEXANDRA: You were brave to try to save that baby. We should go.

HELENE: Alexandra, I was raped by that guard.

(A beat.)

HELENE: I have to go to the camp. Come with me.

(Alexandra doesn't move.)

HELENE: Please come with me.

(Lights shift as Alexandra and Helene approach a dark tent, where inside a woman lies huddled.)

HELENE: It's me, Yvonne.

YVONNE: Helene, you were in jail, no?

HELENE: Alexandra released me. You have to come out and see.

YVONNE: You tried to save my baby, but you cannot save me!

HELENE: Remember the song, Yvonne? (Singing.) "*Chak maten, lè solèy la leve.*" Soon everyone in America will sing it.

YVONNE: You always say you are going to America.

HELENE: I'm still here in Haiti. Come out of the tent.

YVONNE: When my baby drowned, I drowned. I tried to escape, but there is no better life. I like the dark, I got used to the dark--I can breathe in the dark...

HELENE: I want to show you...

YVONNE: I'm like a werewolf, howling in my mind. In the light I'll die, I'll shrivel and die. You want to see me melt in the light of day? Melt like soup?

HELENE: I love soup. Yes. Let's see you melt.

(She pulls Yvonne out into the light.)

HELENE: See the trees, the birds, the blue sky? If you take the top half of the world in Haiti --it is still beautiful. The birds fly as if there is nothing terribly wrong. Where do they go, I sometimes wonder? Do they come back after they leave or are they just passing through?

YVONNE: A bird would *never* come back here! Birds spread the news when they travel: "Haiti is a terrible place, don't go there!" And soon, you'll see, there will be less and less birds until there are none at all, and that will be the end.

HELENE: I've watched them, they do like it here still. They stay for long periods of time, and they do come back and populate the land.

(Helene starts to sing.)

HELENE:
"Chak maten, lè solèy la leve
Nan fenèt mwen, map gade lanmè a

(After a moment, Yvonne begins to sing. Alexandra watches the two women sing as they look up at the light of the sky.)

HELENE/YVONNE:
Mwen se manman lanmè a, bebe mwen!"

SCENE 8:

(Oliver is doing his webcast. It is his way of singing.)

OLIVER: ...If we are tired from hard work and too much noise inside our heads we can sit in the greatest concert hall and listen to a symphony of instruments composed by a great artist who lives on through his notes. We can stand inside ruins that show us past civilizations, which did the unimaginable and we carry the power of their imagination forward. If we are separated from our families, we can find reassurance in their voices and words. We can send messages across countries instantly when before a letter would never arrive. We can take boats across channels and see dawn on the sea all alone in the vastness; watch the sunset peeking through clouds from a plane window. We can taste new dishes that arouse our palates, in the company of people who combine wit and debate like spices. Google what sparks our curiosity--be changed by the ever-rippling surge of collective words. We can save a person through surgery so that a heart beats fine again. Sit in the dark and watch the stars of old with their familiar faces, the ones our parents admired, or watch new ones, whose faces share with us surprising compassion that affirms our own, and bring tears in the dark. Live with our histories and reawaken our old friendships when they might have been forgotten and left behind. All this we can do...because of oil. We are a clever and mutable species. Perhaps one day we'll have something to replace it. For now, it is our gold, the true currency of our civilization. To ignore it is irresponsible. To embrace it is to keep moving forward. I want to congratulate you on your vision, your contribution and your foresight. Thank you for the opportunity to speak to you and for continuing with us on this journey.

SCENE 9:

(Alexandra is in her office with Luz.)

LUZ: The man I worked for told me he could do whatever he liked to me. I don't want to talk about it.

(Luz uses an inhaler for her asthma.)

ALEXANDRA: I know. But in court our government is going to make it seem like you're inventing everything so you can stay in the United States. After your employer found out you were pregnant, what did he do?

LUZ: He blindfolded me and took me to a secret place. It was not a safe operation. That was when my nagual came to me.

ALEXANDRA: *Nagual?*

LUZ: Angel.

ALEXANDRA: Guardian angel. What happened?

LUZ: I was on the table, taking my last breath.

(Lights shift as a Vulture flies onto the table.)

LUZ: My nagual flew down to me. She was always watching. We breathed together.

(She speaks to Vulture.)

LUZ: Mi pequeñita. Mi nagual. (My little one. My nagual.)

(Vulture dips its head down very close to Luz's face, then spreads its wings and flies away. Lights shift back.)

LUZ: When I was examined here, the doctor said I could never have children. It's hard to remember what I lost.

ALEXANDRA: Would your grandmother make a statement about what happened to you? It's key to your case. I'd like to meet with your grandmother in Guatemala. Then she'll speak to an expert witness there. Could you ask your grandmother if she will meet with me?

LUZ: I can ask.

SCENE 10:

(Oliver is with his lawyer, Tim Haskins.)

HASKINS: Matthew Cameron worked with a webmaster who had leanings towards eco-terrorism.

OLIVER: Did those "leanings" ever go anywhere, Haskins?

HASKINS: No, but he's a controversial figure because he's done work with hacker organizations.

OLIVER: So this guy is technically a hacker.

HASKINS: No.

OLIVER: What kind of work did he do for Cameron?

HASKINS: Minimal, one or two work-for-hire jobs. Graphic design.

OLIVER: But he's a hacker?

HASKINS: (A beat.) He used to be more radical when he was younger, Mr. Rausch.

OLIVER: What did he do?

HASKINS: He helped some men who blew up some SUVs.

OLIVER: How did he help them?

HASKINS: Ran the campaign to get them out of jail.

OLIVER: How?

HASKINS: Through a website that was anonymous and suspected of internet vigilantism.

OLIVER: And Cameron hired this hacker?

HASKINS: Yeah, Cameron is listed as one of this guy's accounts, because Cameron is now a rock star.

OLIVER: You are. Let's get something to eat.

SCENE 11:

(Alexandra is with Carmen Ramos, a Guatemalan human rights activist in Guatemala City.)

ALEXANDRA: Carmen...?

CARMEN: I've been lying in a tent for a week. Up every night, too nervous to sleep. They don't like my "Stop-Government-Corruption" banner so I'm not allowed even to use the bathroom in City Hall. I am on a hunger strike and I have to use the Burger King bathroom!

ALEXANDRA: I need you to be my expert witness.

CARMEN: I'm such an "expert" they throw grenades over my wall to shut me up.

ALEXANDRA: My firm will pay for it--we're scheduled in court soon.

CARMEN: I told you already I'm the wrong person! Come back when I'm eating again.

ALEXANDRA: You know a very small percentage of Central Americans get asylum.

CARMEN: (Sarcastic.) Because they are all illiterate peasants and gang members who flee illegally!

ALEXANDRA: Luz has *a well-founded fear* of further persecution. You read the report, what the soldiers did. Her employer.

CARMEN: It's a miracle she survived. The Kaibiles your country trained, they are still in power. (Miming.) Kill people with their bare hands.

ALEXANDRA: Her employer is a former army officer. He's untouchable. And what the U.S. government lawyer will do is argue that he was acting in a private capacity.

CARMEN: Private? Public? What's the difference? Luz's employer would have no obligation to his servant due to her class and ethnicity. 36 years of dirty war has turned women into the enemy. And your country supports our generals who are responsible. Nothing is over--we have dealt with NONE OF IT.

ALEXANDRA: Is that a no?

CARMEN: *You* are working within the system that oppresses us. It's one step forward and one step back. I am sick of it!

ALEXANDRA: The cases I win move the law forward. Luz's life can make a difference.

CARMEN: Why is seeking political asylum *the only way*? Don't you want to make more impact than that? You have to work with the people, on the ground, listen to the people!

ALEXANDRA: Exactly, that's why I'm in Guatemala. I'm going to meet with Luz's grandmother in the basurero. To see if she'll talk to me about what happened during the civil war. We need strong expert testimony, Government is a real "pit bull."

CARMEN: You're going to the basurero?

ALEXANDRA: Yes.

CARMEN: You know all this hunger strike will achieve is to open the door to more talks with the politicians. It's always the poor who lose, it's thankless.

ALEXANDRA: No, it's not.

CARMEN: You know what I'm dreaming about right now, Alexandra?

ALEXANDRA: What?

CARMEN: *Pollo Campero*.

ALEXANDRA: Fried chicken. I admire the work you do, Carmen. I know how hard it is.

CARMEN: You say "Government" is a real *pit bull*?

ALEXANDRA: Yes.

CARMEN: I believe I can last here for another week. I'll think about it.

SCENE 12:

(*Alexandra is with Luz's grandmother, Abuelita, in the garbage dump. They speak in Spanish. Supertiles are used.*)

45

ABUELITA: Yo ya pedí a los dioses por Luz. Puede ofrecerles fruta, encenderles candela, cigarros, agua con colorante…(I made my petition to the gods for Luz. You can give fruit, candles, cigarettes, colored water…)

ALEXANDRA: Que ofreció Ud. para Luz? (What did you offer for Luz?)

ABUELITA: Un pequeño bordado que hizo Luz con su mamá para el huipil. Luz cosió la corona con los escarabajos de fuego para su hermana Tomasa la más chula. Oí lo que alcancé a escuchar. El viento, los pájaros, ellos llevaron a Luz a los Estados Unidos! Oyeron mi petición. Sabe, yo tenía una piedra mágica que daba una luz especial con la cual leía el futuro. Cuando Luz nació, esta piedra me dijo: "Si querés que la niña crezca, que viva, la primera vez que la bañes, pone a cocer un huevo y álzalo encima de la doble corona de su cabecita." Así le hice para que Luz viviera. Pero hubieron otras mujeres en nuestro pueblo que murieron de tristeza. Eso es lo que ocurrió con mi propia hija y mi prima, quien nos ayudó a trabajar acá en el basurero. (A small embroidery Luz made with her mother for the *huipil.* Luz sewed the corona with the fire beetles for her sister Tomasa, the beautiful one. I listened to what I could hear. The wind, the birds, they brought Luz to America! They heard my petition. You see, I had a magic stone that gave off a special light that I used to tell the future. When Luz was born this stone told me: "If you want this girl to grow, to live, when you are first bathing her, cook an egg and hold it over the double crown of her head." This is what I did for Luz to live. But there were women in our village who died of sadness. This is what happened to my own daughter. And to my cousin who helped us to work here in the dump.)

ALEXANDRA: Como puede alguien "morir de tristeza?" (How can you "die of sadness?")

ABUELITA: Cuando llueve, el agua puede llegar a su cuerpo y hacer que sienta frío. Es lo mismo con las lágrimas. Pueden ahogar su corazón tal y como lo hace la lluvia, se ahoga en su propio frío. (When it rains the water can get into your body and make you cold. It's like that with the tears. It can flood your heart like the rain. You drown in your own coldness.)

ALEXANDRA: Porqué no le pasó a usted también? (Why didn't that happen to you?)

ABUELITA: (Laughing.) ¿Por qué sigue respirando? Estoy feliz por Luz que esté en los Estados Unidos. Allí puede ganar mucha plata. Dígame, porqué vino aquí señorita? Soy vieja. Ya casi no recuerdo quién soy. Lo que queremos es enterrar a nuestros muertos! Tendría más suerte de encontrar sus huesos reciclados en este basurero que en nuestro propio pueblo. (Why are you still breathing? I'm happy for Luz that she is in the U.S. She can make lots of money! Why did you come here, lady? I'm old. I barely remember who I am. We want to bury our dead! I have a better chance of finding their bones recycled in this dump than in my own village.)

(Jesus appears. He is rolling a cigarette.)

JESUS: Ah, la gran gringa viene al basurero de visita? Fue el perfume dulce que la sedujo? (Ah, the big *gringa* comes to the garbage dump? Was it the smell that attracted you?)

ALEXANDRA: No comprendo. (I don't understand.)

JESUS: I'll speak English. The smell? You want to put some on a handkerchief to bring home as new perfume? Or maybe you can take some pictures of the swollen babies--maybe the stomachs of the women who give birth to trash--plastic jugs and cardboard? Or, look, photograph the vultures flying down to eat the bones of those who didn't make it. Get your pretty feet wet in the pools of methane. But careful, they might be melting like wax on your way out.

ABUELITA: (To Alexandra.) Este es mi sobrino-nieto Jesus. (To Jesus.) Te dije que no debes fumar aquí, es peligroso. (To Alexandra.) Me ha venido a traer para llevarme a la pollería. (This is my grand-nephew, Jesus. I told you not to smoke here. It's dangerous. He's come to take me to the chicken shop.)

ALEXANDRA: Gracias por su tiempo, abuelita. (Thank you for your time, *abuelita*.)

JESUS: *Abuelita*? Ooohh. D'you read some texts on the native people? Find out about the way we weave on our looms and pat our tortillas.

ALEXANDRA: You speak pretty good English.

JESUS: I went up to Los Angeles — saw all the *"ángeles"* in their cars burnin' up the freeways-- now that place is a *real* dump! Lucky for me I got deported. I'm still connected to my brothers up there. We talk all the time.

ABUELITA: Ya Jesus, Dejala. (Enough, Jesus, leave her alone!)

JESUS: You look like you're part of a L'Oreal ad. L'Oreal's big here. So we can all dye our hair *light*. Hair products and gas stations. That's the future.

ABUELITA: Vonós. (Let's go.)

JESUS: Okay.

(He leaves.)

ALEXANDRA: Gracias. (Thank you.)

ABUELITA: Digale a Luz que necesita olvidar. (Tell Luz she needs to forget.)

SCENE 13:

(Oliver is with his wife Daniela, who shows him a magazine.)

DANIELA: They're taking in Matthew Cameron for questioning.

OLIVER: Lucky for me, they tied Cameron's webmaster to hacking charges.

DANIELA: Mike said Cameron stopped working with that guy a long time ago.

OLIVER: The company's providing extra security. We'll be fine.

DANIELA: It touches on some of your most vulnerable points, doesn't it?

OLIVER: That's what terrorism is meant to do. Even if it's just crazy letters, snail mail, it's designed to make you afraid.

(Daniela reads from the magazine.)

DANIELA: "There once was a guy who loved oil
And to the death of mankind he was loyal
When his son did call out
This asshole did shout
I love to watch your rare turtles boil!"
You've seen it. (A beat.) It's funny.

OLIVER: It was brought to my attention. Mike sent the poem into the campaign, signed it.

DANIELA: You didn't say anything?

OLIVER: I asked them to respond the way we always respond.

DANIELA: You sent your son a form letter. How did the magazine get the limerick?

OLIVER: Mike sent a copy to Matthew Cameron. I can't believe they would publish it. It's terrible!

DANIELA: Your son's crying out to you.

OLIVER: Well, this won't help.

DANIELA: You're running, Ollie.

OLIVER: (Trying to joke.) No time to run...

DANIELA: You wake up in a panic in the middle of the night.

OLIVER: Stress. I don't want to talk about it. Look at the view. Can you believe this view?

DANIELA: But something's there, you won't let out.

OLIVER: Is that why *you* run around the world screaming your lungs out? To let it out for me?

DANIELA: Maybe. It's so beautiful to sing. To let it out. I'm a singer--I love my art. I rehearse--my time is filled with that. How can I think about the rest?

OLIVER: I stopped singing.

DANIELA: Love can't always get you through.

OLIVER: (Kissing her.) I love you so much. Mike loves you so much. We're a mutual worshipping society to you.

DANIELA: But to each other? You always keep your distance with him. Push him away. You're so formal, aloof. What are you afraid of?

OLIVER: I want to protect him.

DANIELA: From what?

OLIVER: The whole goddamn world, Daniela.

DANIELA: You can't, baby.

OLIVER: I will.

DANIELA: You're a good man. Take a step. Any step.

OLIVER: What step?

DANIELA: Listen to Mike. Talk to him. He needs you.

OLIVER: Does he really believe in this turtle stuff or is he just doing it to piss me off?

DANIELA: Ask him.

OLIVER: What would happen if I quit? (Looking around.) Then he wouldn't have all of this. The trips we take...

DANIELA: Do you want to?

OLIVER: That train has left the station...

DANIELA: Go back to science?

OLIVER: We're on it. We couldn't change our lives if we tried! And yet there's this fantasy that keeps liberals alive--the fantasy of liberal guilt. That if you feel GUILT you're solving the problem! That pisses me off more than anything!

DANIELA: I've heard this...

OLIVER: That's what I want my son to know. There is no better *truth* than this!

DANIELA: He's heard that already, Oliver, your speech. What about something new?

OLIVER: And I've heard about his turtles and his eggs and his "little tracks the mothers make when they go from the nest into the gulf." I don't care!

DANIELA: But you're the father, Oliver. You should have told me he was writing to you through your company.

OLIVER: It was a fucking limerick, Daniela! Couldn't he have written a sonnet? Something a little more elevated than that lowbrow humor.

DANIELA: If he writes a limerick, you want a sonnet. But if he writes a sonnet, you want twitter. You want what he doesn't have because he's pushing your buttons...

OLIVER: He's a stupid kid, go ahead and have your love fest then, Daniela!

DANIELA: Maybe there's something in between your shame and his turtles?

OLIVER: I don't have any shame. You can't have what we have and have any relief from it.

SCENE 14:

(*Carmen Ramos, the expert witness, is with Alexandra and Luz in Alexandra's office. Alexandra wears her dress for court.*)

CARMEN: I came for *you*, Luz. You are the real pit bull. And *I* am the true authority on pit bulls, let me assure you. And so is your grandmother.

LUZ: Thank you?

CARMEN: When I went to visit her in the dump she made me laugh!

LUZ: Why?

CARMEN: The stories she told me!

LUZ: You know, sometimes it's not true, she imagines. It's all in her head.

CARMEN: What else do we have but our imagination?

ALEXANDRA: Your case is in very good shape, Luz. I've asked the judge for a closed proceeding. One question at a time, we'll take breaks. If the government lawyer, Mr. Colby, tries to confuse you, look at the judge.

LUZ: What if I can't remember?

ALEXANDRA: You can remember. And, Carmen, *you* must remember that even though you're music to my ears, our courts have very little patience.

CARMEN: My signal to "kiss ass!"

(Tim Haskins enters.)

HASKINS: Can I talk to you a minute, Alexa?

CARMEN: We'll meet you downstairs.

(Alexandra quickly opens a shoebox. Carmen and Luz exit.)

HASKINS: Look at you.

ALEXANDRA: I always dress this way for court. You know that.

HASKINS: You're a woman, and you'll fight like one. No Banana Republic suits for you.

ALEXANDRA: No, I haven't even had time to make sure they go with the dress. Are you okay?

(She begins to try on the shoes.)

HASKINS: Matthew Cameron wants the bird deterrents to be completely removed because he says they're not working. And now he and the indigenous people are fighting for the tailings facilities to go too.

ALEXANDRA: Wasn't Cameron brought up on some charges?

HASKINS: The hacking charges were a bad idea.

ALEXANDRA: Whose bad idea?

HASKINS: I take the fifth. Mr. Rausch on the other hand claims this new batch of bird deaths are because of the *weather*.

ALEXANDRA: Now, you're referring to dead birds in "batches?"

HASKINS: He says they're dying because of freezing rains. The poor birds are so exhausted from the weight of the freezing rain on their feathers they're forced to land on the ponds even though the deterrents are working fine. And to top it off, Matthew Cameron's started media-hyped demonstrations with the indigenous people.

ALEXANDRA: You look a little green around the gills.

HASKINS: *Fish* are dying too, Alexa, we're not out of the woods. Speaking of *woods*, massive quantities of carbon dioxide are killing trees. I'm not sure where this is going to stop.

ALEXANDRA: There is a point where the law stops and what happens is totally outside our control. The outcome depends on whether we have the strength to tell the story and whether the judge will hear it. It's about risk and fallacy. It's impossible to feel any certainty. It's impossible to feel any ego, to distinguish between legal advocacy and that much less definite feeling of raw hope that we must win, because we cannot lose.

(*He looks at her, now that she has the shoes on.*)

HASKINS: They go with the dress.
ALEXANDRA: Thank you.

SCENE 15:

(*Mr. Colby questions Carmen Ramos, and Judge Mary Hurst presides. Alexandra and Luz watch as Carmen spells out a name.*)

CARMEN: I-N-O-C-E-N-T-A and U-S.
MR. COLBY: U-S?
CARMEN: Yes.
MR. COLBY: How do you know it's a Mayan name?
CARMEN: Because Inocenta Us is Mayan. You are familiar with the REHMI report on the civil war?
MR. COLBY: Ms. Ramos...
CARMEN: Good, then you know that the army targeted Mayan women during the genocide. Inocenta Us was forced to run away with her granddaughter, Luz Lopez.
MR. COLBY: According to Ms. Lopez's grandmother, how many soldiers were involved?
CARMEN: She said she saw Luz "gang-raped" by two men.
MR. COLBY: The grandmother could do nothing to stop this?
CARMEN: This was brutal, systematic killing.
MR. COLBY: She couldn't call for help?
CARMEN: No, it was a campaign of terror.

MR. COLBY: Did she tell you this, or is it common knowledge?

CARMEN: She told me this and it is common knowledge.

MR. COLBY: Really?

CARMEN: It did not make any difference if she "called for help."

MR. COLBY: When did you first meet the respondent?

CARMEN: I met Luz Lopez earlier today.

MR. COLBY: Can you tell the difference between a Mayan person and a *mestizo*, a mix of European and Indian?

CARMEN: Yes.

MR. COLBY: Does she look Mayan?

CARMEN: Yes.

MR. COLBY: Do I look Mayan?

CARMEN: No!

MR. COLBY: What makes her look Mayan?

CARMEN: Her nose, she has classic Mayan features-- she speaks the language.

MR. COLBY: She speaks Spanish?

CARMEN: She speaks Spanish and Mam.

MR. COLBY: Mam?

CARMEN: Mam is her native language.

MR. COLBY: Why do you think the arrival of one person in a city with a population of 3 million would be noticed?

CARMEN: Because her employer would know when she returns.

MR. COLBY: Would she be safe in another city?

CARMEN: It doesn't' matter where she goes!

MR. COLBY: Why not?

CARMEN: Femicide.

MR. COLBY: And what, in your opinion, is the definition of "femicide"?

CARMEN: The epidemic of woman-killing is the combination of soaring crime rates, government corruption, drug cartels from Mexico and the rise of youth gangs...

MR. COLBY: Thank you...

CARMEN: It is also combined with cultural aspects like the patriarchal, male-dominated society...

MR. COLBY: Thank you.

CARMEN: And the training of death squads--women are found killed the same way-- (Miming.) Rope around neck. The proof is in the dead bodies.

MR. COLBY: Thank you, Ms. Ramos. That's all I have.

JUDGE HURST: Redirect on cross-examination, counsel.

ALEXANDRA: Thank you, Your Honor. When you spoke to Ms. Lopez's grandmother, did she mention to you any words used by the military soldiers when they gang-raped Luz Lopez, Ms. Ramos?

CARMEN: "Indio."

ALEXANDRA: What does Indio mean?

CARMEN: It is referring to Ms. Lopez's ethnicity of Mayan.

ALEXANDRA: When the former army officer who abused Ms. Lopez as a domestic used the words "Too dark to be beautiful" and "*We* like white meat" what did this mean?

CARMEN: The indigenous is not human like the white skinned, but is the savage, the animal to be debased, buried, and stuck in a mass grave to burn.

SCENE 16:

(*Oliver suddenly hears "O Fortuna" of Carmina Burana. A male singer, who plays the Roasted Swan in the opera, haunts him in his dream.*)

ROASTED SWAN: (Singing.) "*Oliver, enclosed my missive. Don't be dismissive…*"

OLIVER: Don't write me a letter! Sing your comic aria and get offstage.

ROASTED SWAN: I was flying across the sky, stopped to rest on a toxic slick. You're talking to…

OLIVER: The Roasted Swan, I know, Daniela has sung *Carmina Burana* dozens of times! Even did the recording for the car commercial.

ROASTED SWAN: Cars run on *oil*.

OLIVER: I've always found your character lowbrow!

ROASTED SWAN: Oh and your smear campaign wasn't lowbrow?

OLIVER: Cameron had links to that hacker.

ROASTED SWAN: None were proven.

OLIVER: You sound like my son. "You just sink lower and lower, dad!"

ROASTED SWAN: He's right. Cameron has gone viral.

OLIVER: The letters are dwindling--Cameron isn't even getting his 15 minutes. I'm starving.

ROASTED SWAN: Ah, I made you hungry. Art inspires! Well, the Russian Tea Room doesn't serve *Roasted Swan*.

OLIVER: I get turkey.

ROASTED SWAN: (Singing.) "I see bared teeth." Yours.

OLIVER: Just get eaten and go!

ROASTED SWAN: I'm stuck, Oliver. I can't move. My legs are sinking in tar. I put out my wings to fly and I can't take off. That motion of flying. Getting away. Haven't you ever been stuck under the weight of some terrible power?

OLIVER: I'm all light. Just look at the windows.

(They look at the windows. The swan can't fly.)

ROASTED SWAN: Look at the birds. At the light. Can you see it?

SCENE 17:

(Mr. Colby is interviewing Luz. Alexandra and Judge Hurst watch.)

MR. COLBY: How many brothers did you have in your native village, Ms. Lopez?

LUZ: Two, taken away by the men who came to our door.

MR. COLBY: And then, allegedly, Ms. Lopez, *two more* men came to your door? Who were those men? I know this was all very, very long ago. Do you even remember? What were these men wearing?

ALEXANDRA: Objection--he's badgering the witness, Your Honor.

(The judge intercedes.)

JUDGE HURST: Ms. Lopez, who came to the door?

LUZ: The army.

JUDGE HURST: How did you know the men were from the army?

LUZ: The two men wore military uniforms.

JUDGE HURST: Counselor, please move forward.

MR. COLBY: Thank you, Your Honor. Who was in the house when the men came to the door, as you say?

LUZ: My father, mother, grandmother and sister.

MR. COLBY: What did the men do, Ms. Lopez?

LUZ: They ate my mother's food. My father asked them to go.

MR. COLBY: Your father asked them to go where?

LUZ: They started to beat me.

MR. COLBY: Did the men go?

LUZ: No.

MR. COLBY: Did they beat your mother too?

LUZ: No.

MR. COLBY: What happened to your sister?

LUZ: She hid.

MR. COLBY: Did you hide?

LUZ: It was too late.

MR. COLBY: But your sister hid!

LUZ: Yes.

MR. COLBY: Why was it too late for you to hide, Ms. Lopez?

LUZ: There was only time to hide my sister.

MR. COLBY: Were you even raped by the men, Ms. Lopez? Or is that just something you heard happened to other women in your village? Did you hear about other women being raped in your village by the military?

ALEXANDRA: Objection, Your Honor!

JUDGE HURST: Sustained. Counselor, move on, please.

LUZ: Yes, everyone heard. The army raped the women in our village.

MR. COLBY: Could you be recalling something that happened to other women, ma'am?

ALEXANDRA: Objection!

JUDGE HURST: (To Alexandra.) Counsel.

LUZ: (Shaking.) I was raped by two military men.

MR. COLBY: Later after you left the garbage dump in Guatemala City, you worked as a"domestic." Did you report the alleged abuse by your employer to the police?

LUZ: If I screamed I thought the gardener might hear. But then I would be punished. I didn't scream.

MR. COLBY: How long after he began to abuse you did you become pregnant?

LUZ: Six months.

MR. COLBY: But I don't understand Ms. Lopez, you worked for this army officer for many years...?

(A beat.)

JUDGE HURST: Please continue, Ms. Lopez.

LUZ: He began to abuse me after his wife died. I begged the man performing the abortion to call for help. He left me alone. Finally, my master came back and put me in a car. He stopped raping me but continued to beat and punch me. I saved money to come to the U.S.

MR. COLBY: Where on your body did he beat you?

LUZ: The stomach. The breasts. The thighs. (Turning to Judge Hurst.) Judge I would like to talk to you.

JUDGE HURST: Ms. Lopez, you have an attorney representing you.

ALEXANDRA: Your Honor, I'd like to request a break.

JUDGE HURST: Yes, counselor, I think that's very appropriate.

(Luz stands up.)

LUZ: I cannot speak about these things to a person who is not looking at me. He is not even looking in my direction.

ALEXANDRA: Your Honor, we need to take a break.

LUZ: I would like to request that he look at me when he speaks to me. He is not giving me the respect I deserve simply as another human being. I will not continue until he looks at me!

JUDGE HURST: Counselor, I request that you please quiet your client…

MR. COLBY: I doubt Ms. Lopez's credibility, Your Honor. There are areas that are inconsistent.

JUDGE HURST: The court will take a recess!

(Judge Hurst and Mr. Colby exit.)

ALEXANDRA: You were doing so well, Luz. What happened?

LUZ: You prepared me for this?

ALEXANDRA: His job is to destroy your credibility.

LUZ: How can you destroy something that's already been destroyed?

ALEXANDRA: You are not destroyed--this is a good judge, Luz. She'll understand that you needed a moment to calm down.

LUZ: This is torture.

SCENE 18:

(Alexandra's phone beeps and she looks at it. Lights rise on Helene in the camp in Haiti, with a Reporter. Helene is holding her stomach.)

REPORTER: Live Twitter Report, Camp Cité Soleil, Haiti. (Sending the message.) Tweet.

HELENE: As soon as I saw the pregnancy stick at the clinic, I knew…

REPORTER: Helene LaForet. Tweet.

HELENE: I would take the pills.

REPORTER: Took oxytocin. Tweet.

HELENE: Not enough food for me--none for a newborn. My womb is contracting like a trampoline!

REPORTER: We need to get her to a hospital. Tweet.

HELENE: I feel like I'm going to faint.

(The reporter helps her to lie down.)

REPORTER: I'm going to call for help. Try to breathe.

(He makes a phone call.)

REPORTER: (On phone.) Yes! I'm a reporter, in Cité Soleil…I'll hold.

(She screams.)

HELENE: This is not an immaculate conception.

REPORTER: No, no.

(Helene looks up at the sky. She hears birds.)

HELENE: Do you know birds?

REPORTER: (Trying to comfort her.) Yes, I do, I do.

HELENE: Where do they go, I sometimes wonder?

(*The reporter closes Helene's eyes.*)

REPORTER: 3:03 PM. Tweet.

SCENE 19:

(*Alexandra in darkness looks down at Helene's dead body. Alexandra is barefoot.*)

ALEXANDRA: I wasn't there, Helene.

(*Alexandra looks up at the narrow window from her dream of before, where the beam of light streams through.*)

ALEXANDRA: I see the trees, the birds, the blue sky.

(*Zia enters. She looks at Alexandra.*)

ZIA: Why are you running without your shoes?

(*Alexandra looks up at the narrow window.*)

ALEXANDRA: I can't get in.

(*Zia looks up at the narrow window, speaking in Sudanese. Supertitles are used.*)

ZIA: Anna laheena laheenak. (Miss In-Between?)

ALEXANDRA: Yes. The window always gets smaller and smaller

(Luz appears.)

LUZ: Pero la mitad del mundo sigue allí. (But the top half of the world is still there.)

(The flutter of wings. The Vulture nagual flies in and lands near Luz.)

ZIA: A-ttyoour beetarjaa. (The birds do come back.)
LUZ: Sabés? Los zopes solían asustarme en el basurero. Su forma de mirarme... Siempre pensé: "están esperando que yo muera." Pero cuando miro a mi nagual sé que todos los seres han sido puestos en la tierra para ser amados. Ya no tengo miedo. El amor se encuentra incluso en los lugares más oscuros y nos guiará a través de la estrecha ventana. Siempre. (You know the vultures used to scare me in the dump. The way they watched me. I kept on thinking they're waiting for me to die. But when I look at my nagual I know that all beings are put on earth to be loved. I'm not afraid anymore. Love can be found in the darkest places and that will lead us upward through the narrowest window forever.)

(The Vulture nagual flies away. Helene sits up.)

HELENE: Se somb. (It's dark.)

ALEXANDRA: I like the dark, I'm used to the dark--I can breathe in the dark.

HELENE: Mwen te rele bebe mwen an "Lespwa." (I named the baby inside of me Lespwa.)

ALEXANDRA: "Lespwa"?

HELENE: It means "Hope." I named my baby "Hope" because she is my story.

ZIA: What is your story, Alexandra?

HELENE: Tell us your story.

LUZ: Cuéntanos tu historia. (Tell us your story.)

(Zia, Helene and Luz watch Alexandra, as she stares up at the narrow window.)

ALEXANDRA: I was 17. The restaurant where I worked, we'd go a bunch of us to a bar. I didn't drink much. One of the men, his name was David--we decided to take a cab down to a club to go dancing. I loved to dance. He said he had to stop at his house to get a jacket. I didn't want to stop but he insisted. We go into his apartment. I don't exactly remember where it was. An older man comes in. He's cutting up cocaine with a razor blade. He's very high. He tells me to do some cocaine--I say no, I'm going to leave. There's a guard dog, barking. The man says, "Don't leave." I'm afraid to run and get attacked by the dog. He takes my hand and says, "Let me read your palm." He moves his hand up my arm and grips it. "Take off your clothes." He takes me upstairs to a loft. When the older guy is raping me, I see a window. He tells David to rape me. He doesn't do it as hard. The older man has sex with me again and again. At morning, dawn, a man comes in, he's angry at me. He tells me to go. I'm able to leave.

(*She looks down at her bare feet.*)

I walked home without my shoes. That's what I remember. I didn't tell anyone. When I looked up at the window, I was watching myself.

(*The women all look up at the narrow window.*)

SCENE 20:

(*Oliver, outside a courthouse, looking at his phone, approaches Matthew Cameron, who has take-out coffee. Oliver shakes Matthew's hand.*)

OLIVER: I couldn't resist stopping, to say hello.
MATTHEW: Hello.
OLIVER: Last time we spoke face to face it was about snail mail.
MATTHEW: Guess the people want my message to travel faster these days.
OLIVER: Well, I'll be sharing the good news with the shareholders.
MATTHEW: Yeah, what's 600 million dollars to them?

OLIVER: Look, we are just thankful we can provide a cleanup your people will be satisfied with.

MATTHEW: Who said anything about satisfaction, Mr. Rausch?

OLIVER: The lawyers.

MATTHEW: It's not over yet.

OLIVER: What is your vision? I really want to know. What would happen if we couldn't go across the street to get our take-out coffee? If all the lights went out?

MATTHEW: Something *better*.

OLIVER: We share the same belief.

MATTHEW: Are you practicing your "spin" on me?

OLIVER: So what's next for you?

MATTHEW: Press conference. The indigenous are still being driven off their land, being exterminated.

OLIVER: Oh yes, so you're going to release a bunch of vultures to eat carcasses of dead birds and call it a native ceremony?

MATTHEW: The indigenous people call it *Nature*, it's beautiful. They're reclaiming what's theirs.

OLIVER: I call it a sensational show for the sake of the cameras.

MATTHEW: Real vultures are scavengers, Oliver. They clean up the earth, like water, the earth's miracle. Do you remember what *water* is?

OLIVER: Molecule made up of one oxygen, two hydrogen atoms connected by covalent bonds — the universal solvent. I believe in science. We are working every day to find alternatives. It's exciting to learn about new discoveries. And it's equally exciting for me to learn how to find solutions to the obstacles. I *love* that dichotomy.

MATTHEW: Your obstacles are outpacing your solutions.

OLIVER: I know--I feel like one of my son's turtles. (Referring to his phone.) I got a major debacle in Guatemala City. Huge explosion at one of our gas stations, spread to the garbage dump down below. Towering inferno. (He puts his phone away.) I'm developing a new foundation and to get it started in the right direction, we need people with vision and I'm hoping to integrate…

MATTHEW: Are you offering me a job?

OLIVER: Think about it.

SCENE 21:

(Alexandra is in her office and outside her office there is a law firm party. Haskins enters with two glasses.)

HASKINS: Congratulations.

ALEXANDRA: Congratulations to you.

HASKINS: They really pulled out all the stops.

ALEXANDRA: Because of your oil win.

HASKINS: And Ms. Lopez.

ALEXANDRA: You know this isn't because of Ms. Lopez.

HASKINS: Your win is where the prestige comes from. Toast?

71

ALEXANDRA: My clients fulfill the firm's Corporate Social Responsibility. A warped tit for tat where the ones being abused actually *absolve* our firm and the corporations. You and I just keep canceling each other out. That's no reason to toast.

HASKINS: She's not an *alien* anymore.

ALEXANDRA: How do you live with yourself?

HASKINS: Matthew Cameron, the freezing rains, the fish, the bark on the trees melting, I didn't think we were going to find a way to settle.

ALEXANDRA: I meant how does *one* live with oneself? It wasn't an attack.

HASKINS: We don't cancel each other out, Alexa. The gray areas where we can argue, it starts there.

ALEXANDRA: Who actually *tells* the truth, that's one gray area for me.

HASKINS: Are you talking about oil?

ALEXANDRA: No. The truth isn't always for public consumption.

HASKINS: But that's your job, to expose the truth for your clients and win them *safety* in the U.S.!

ALEXANDRA: And what's the value of *safety* if the perpetrator never goes away?

HASKINS: A way out of the dark. A refuge.

(*Alexandra raises her glass.*)

ALEXANDRA: The gray areas. Let's toast to them...to trying to get to the other side.

(They clink glasses. Lights shift to Luz and Alexandra in a park. Luz eats chocolate.)

LUZ: It's a big building. There are many offices. I clean at night, as quickly as possible. In and out. Some of the rooms have fish in water tanks. Blue. They ask me to feed the fish. Thank you for the chocolate. It's delicious.

ALEXANDRA: You're welcome.

(They stand and take in the park. We hear birds.)

ALEXANDRA: The trees are nice. It's peaceful.

LUZ: It's safe.

ALEXANDRA: Yes.

LUZ: Alexandra?

ALEXANDRA: Hum?

LUZ: I spoke to abuelita on the phone. Jesus held people hostage at the gas station.

ALEXANDRA: At the dump?

LUZ: When the police came he set the tanks on fire.

ALEXANDRA: Is he okay?

LUZ: Yes.

ALEXANDRA: It's awful to have to live like that in the trash. The smell stayed on me for days after I left.

LUZ: The people need the dump to survive.

ALEXANDRA: So what will happen to him?

LUZ: Abuelita will visit him every week. He and the gangs control the jails. They will build an even bigger

73

gas station at the top. And Jesus will have to fight harder with larger explosions. I think about it.

ALEXANDRA: What?

LUZ: He wasn't always that way…I'm not there anymore…

(*The flutter of birds' wings. Alexandra looks up.*)

LUZ: But I can still see it.

END OF PLAY

Haitian Creole Translations/Pronunciations:

SONG:

"Chak maten, lè solèy la leve"
Shahk mah-ten, leh so-LEY la lev-eh
"Nan fenèt mwen, map gade lanmè a"
Nahn fuh-NET mwehn, mahp gad-eh la MAY-ah
"Mwen se manman lanmè a, bebe mwen !"
Mwehn say mahn-mahn la MAY-ah, baybay mwehn!

English:
"Every morning, When the sun rises, At my window, I look at the sea, I am the mother of the sea, my baby."

Catherine Filloux is an award-winning playwright, whose more than twenty plays have been produced in the U.S. and around the world. Her play *Luz* premiered at La MaMa in New York City, where she is an Artist in Residence, and was then produced at Looking for Lilith in Louisville, Kentucky. *Selma '65,* her new play about the civil rights movement and the KKK, is also a new La MaMa production. Catherine was invited on an overseas reading tour to Sudan and South Sudan organized by the University of Iowa's International Writing Program; and her play *The Beauty Inside* was produced in Northern Iraq, in the Kurdish language, by ArtRole. Filloux has been commissioned by the Wiener Staatsoper (Vienna State Opera House) to write the libretto for a new opera, which will premiere in 2019. She is the librettist for *The Floating Box* (Music by Jason Kao Hwang), *Where Elephants Weep* (Music by Sophy Him) and *New Arrivals* (Music by John Glover). Filloux's plays are published by Playscripts, Smith & Kraus, Vintage, DPS and Prentice Hall. Her anthologies include *Silence of God and Other Plays*, published by Seagull Books, and *Dog and Wolf & Killing the Boss*, NoPassport Press. Catherine received her M.F.A. in Dramatic Writing from Tisch School of the Arts at N.Y.U. and her French Baccalaureate in Philosophy with Honors in Toulon, France. Filloux is featured in the documentary film "Acting Together on the World Stage" co-created by Dr. Cynthia E. Cohen and filmmaker Allison Lund. She is a co-founder of Theatre Without Borders and has served as a speaker for playwriting and human rights organizations around the world. Catherine deeply thanks all those in her life who have so generously supported her and collaborated with her, without them there would be no books. http://www.catherinefilloux.com

NoPassport

NoPassport is a Pan-American theatre alliance & press devoted to live, virtual and print action, advocacy and change toward the fostering of cross-cultural diversity in the arts with an emphasis on the embrace of the hemispheric spirit in US Latina/o and Latin-American theatre-making.

NoPassport Press' Dreaming the Americas Series and Theatre & Performance PlayTexts Series promotes new writing for the stage, texts on theory and practice and theatrical translations.

Series Editors:

Randy Gener, Jorge Huerta, Mead Hunter, Otis Ramsey-Zoe, Stephen Squibb, Caridad Svich

Advisory Board:

Daniel Banks, Amparo Garcia-Crow, Maria M. Delgado, Elana Greenfield, Christina Marin, Antonio Ocampo

Guzman, Sarah Cameron Sunde, Saviana Stanescu,
Tamara Underiner, Patricia Ybarra

NoPassport is a sponsored project of Fractured Atlas. Tax-deductible donations to NoPassport to fund future publications, conferences and performance events may be made directly to
http://www.fracturedatlas.org/donate/2623

9 781312 206144

CPSIA information can be obtained
at www.ICGtesting.com
Printed in the USA
LVHW042247021221
705104LV00015B/1554

9 781312 206144